STANDARD OF EXCELLENCE
Advanced Jazz Ensemble Method
FOR GROUP OR INDIVIDUAL INSTRUCTION

BY DEAN SORENSON & BRUCE PEARSON

Dear Student:

Welcome to the STANDARD OF EXCELLENCE ADVANCED JAZZ ENSEMBLE METHOD. The jazz tradition is rich and varied, calling many styles of music its own. This book is divided into three sections, each representing a different jazz style: **Swing**, **Latin**, and **Rock**. The three sections are color-coded:

- ◆ The **Swing** section is indicated by   tabs and graphics.

- ◆ The **Latin** section is indicated by   tabs and graphics.

- ◆ The **Rock** section is indicated by   tabs and graphics.

Each section contains IMPROVISATION STUDIES, ADVANCED IMPROVISATION STUDIES, and SUGGESTED SOLOS that may be played with other members of the jazz ensemble, or with the CD included with this book. Each new collection of exercises is marked by   in the Swing section,   in the Latin section, and   in the Rock section. The CD track number for each exercise is indicated by an icon and number (for example: ◎3). Further information about the CD is included on Track 1.

Each section of the book also includes charts designed to be performed by the full jazz ensemble. The charts allow you to apply what you learn in the corresponding exercises.

Careful and diligent practice of the materials in this book will help you further develop your jazz performance skills, especially as an improviser, giving you the tools necessary to explore even more advanced techniques. We wish you a rewarding musical journey!

Sincerely,

Dean Sorenson

Bruce Pearson

ISBN 0-8497-2556-9

KJOS NEIL A. KJOS MUSIC COMPANY, PUBLISHER

W35TP2

IMPROVISATION STUDIES – RIVER CITY BLUES

BLUES SCALE

RIVER CITY BLUES is based on the **blues scale** and the **12-bar blues** — the most common form in jazz.

The series of chords that accompanies a melody is called a **chord progression.** Tunes based on the blues usually have a **blues chord progression** (or simply, **blues progression**). The blues scale is a good starting point when improvising over the blues progression because any note of the scale can be played over any chord of the progression in the same key as the scale.

RIVER CITY BLUES is a **swing** tune. When improvising, choose rhythms in that same style for your solos. Develop the necessary rhythm vocabulary by listening to accomplished jazz musicians play in a swing style. CD Tracks 3-10 provide some examples.

▶ IMPROVISATION STUDY A is a C blues (Concert B♭ blues) scale played in a swing style.
▶ Strive to match the phrasing and articulation of the trumpet, tenor sax, and trombone on the recording.

▶ These **licks** (melodic patterns) are derived from the C blues (Concert B♭ blues) scale, and are played in a swing style.
▶ Listen carefully to the tenor sax on the recording. Be sure to match the player's phrasing and articulation.

IMPROVISATION STUDIES – RIVER CITY BLUES, cont.

▶ These licks are derived from the C blues (Concert B♭ blues) scale, and are played in a swing style.

You are now ready to solo on RIVER CITY BLUES. Use the SUGGESTED SOLO on page 5 as a starting point, or continue with the ADVANCED IMPROVISATION STUDIES.

ADVANCED IMPROVISATION STUDIES – RIVER CITY BLUES

Call and response is a performance style in which musicians carry on a back-and-forth musical dialogue. The **call** is a musical statement or question, and the **response** provides a musical answer.

▶ In the bars with slashes, use swing rhythms combined with pitches from the C blues scale to create responses to the calls the first time. The second time, improvise the entire **chorus**.

To be a good improviser, you need to rely on your ears. The ultimate goal is to be able to hear improvisations in your head, then play them back instantaneously on your instrument. One way to develop that skill is to echo licks played by someone else.

C2 EAR OPENERS

▶ Listen to each lick, then echo it on your instrument. As you play, echo not only the pitches and rhythms, but also the phrasing and articulation exactly as you hear them. This is called **playing by ear**.
▶ The pitch shown is your starting pitch for all of the licks in this exercise.

When soloing on RIVER CITY BLUES, use the SUGGESTED SOLO on page 5 as a model.
For additional improvisation practice, use the SUGGESTED SOLO as an IMPROVISATION STUDY.

River City Blues

SUGGESTED SOLO – RIVER CITY BLUES

The SUGGESTED SOLO is intended as a model. Once you learn it, you may choose to perform it as written during the RIVER CITY BLUES solo section (bars 41-52). You are encouraged, however, to improvise a solo, even if your improvisation is largely based on the SUGGESTED SOLO.

To use the SUGGESTED SOLO as an IMPROVISATION STUDY with the CD, listen to the solo the first time, play the solo the second time, and improvise the third and fourth times.

▶ The SUGGESTED SOLO is constructed of licks derived from the **C BLUES** (Concert B♭ blues) scale. Licks from **IMPROV STUDY B** (IMPROVISATION STUDY B) are also included. This is shown by the **analysis** beneath the music.

IMPROVISATION STUDIES – OINK JOINT RUMBLE

BLUES SCALE

The blues influences every type of jazz in some way. Blues scale **fragments** (portions) are commonly used by jazz players when improvising on non-blues progressions. This is especially true when the progression is made up of **dominant seventh chords**, like G7 and F7 (Concert F7 and E♭7) in the OINK JOINT RUMBLE solo section.

To use blues scale fragments when improvising, you can often simply play notes from the blues scale built on the **tonic note** of the tune or solo section. The tonic note corresponds to the letter name of the key. For example, OINK JOINT RUMBLE and its solo section are in the key of G (Concert F), and you can use the G blues (Concert F blues) scale over all chords in the progression.

OINK JOINT RUMBLE is a swing tune. When improvising, choose rhythms in that same style for your solos. Develop the necessary rhythm vocabulary by listening to accomplished jazz musicians play in a swing style. CD Tracks 11-18 provide some examples.

SWING ♩ = 108–120

▶ IMPROVISATION STUDY A is a G blues (Concert F blues) scale played in a swing style.
▶ Strive to match the phrasing and articulation of the trumpet, tenor sax, and trombone on the recording.

▶ These licks are derived from the G blues (Concert F blues) scale, and are played in a swing style.

You are now ready to solo on OINK JOINT RUMBLE. Use the SUGGESTED SOLO on page 9 as a starting point, or continue with the ADVANCED IMPROVISATION STUDIES.

ADVANCED IMPROVISATION STUDIES – OINK JOINT RUMBLE

DOMINANT SEVENTH CHORDS

While scales are often used as a pitch set for improvisation, the use of **chord tones** is also common. In OINK JOINT RUMBLE, use G7 and F7 chord tones as indicated by the chord symbols.

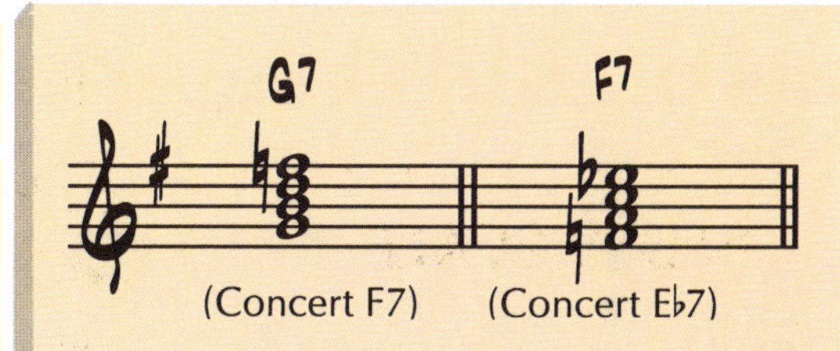

C1 (LISTEN 1ST TIME, PLAY 2ND TIME) 14

MIXOLYDIAN SCALES

In addition to using blues scales over dominant seventh chords, improvisers often use **mixolydian scales**. In OINK JOINT RUMBLE, use G mixolydian over G7 and F mixolydian over F7.

C2 (LISTEN 1ST TIME, PLAY 2ND TIME) 15

C3 CALL AND RESPONSE 16

▶ In the bars with slashes, use swing rhythms combined with chord and scale tones from ADVANCED IMPROVISATION STUDIES C1 and C2 to create responses to the calls the first time. The second time, improvise the entire chorus.

C4 EAR OPENERS 17

▶ Listen to each lick, then echo it on your instrument.
▶ The first pitch shown is your starting pitch for the first two licks. The second pitch is your starting pitch for the third and fourth licks. Let your ears determine the starting pitches for the remaining licks.

When soloing on OINK JOINT RUMBLE, use the SUGGESTED SOLO on page 9 as a model. For additional improvisation practice, use the SUGGESTED SOLO as an IMPROVISATION STUDY.

Oink Joint Rumble

SUGGESTED SOLO – OINK JOINT RUMBLE

The SUGGESTED SOLO is intended as a model. Once you learn it, you may choose to perform it as written during the OINK JOINT RUMBLE solo section (bars 53-68). You are encouraged, however, to improvise a solo, even if your improvisation is largely based on the SUGGESTED SOLO.

To use the SUGGESTED SOLO as an IMPROVISATION STUDY with the CD, listen to the solo the first time, play the solo the second time, and improvise the third and fourth times.

▶ The SUGGESTED SOLO is constructed of licks derived from the G BLUES (Concert F blues) scale, G and F MIXOLYDIAN (Concert F and E♭ mixolydian) scales, and G7 and F7 (Concert F7 and E♭7) CHORD TONES.

▶ If you bypassed the ADVANCED IMPROVISATION STUDIES on page 7, you may be unfamiliar with some of the chords and scales used in this solo. Review the ADVANCED IMPROVISATION STUDIES to learn more about these musical elements, or simply use the solo's pitches, rhythms, and licks as a starting point for your own improvisation.

IMPROVISATION STUDIES – MINOR ATTITUDE

DORIAN SCALE

The **dorian scale** is a common choice when improvising over **minor seventh chords**, like Dmi7 and Emi7 (Concert Cmi7 and Dmi7) in the MINOR ATTITUDE solo section.

Even though the chords in the solo section alternate between Dmi7 and Emi7, the **tonality** (key center) of the section is simply D minor (Concert C minor). The addition of Emi7 adds harmonic interest, but does not change the Dmi7 character of the groove. Therefore, D dorian (Concert C dorian) may be used over the entire solo section.

MINOR ATTITUDE is a swing tune. When improvising, choose rhythms in that same style for your solos. Develop the necessary rhythm vocabulary by listening to accomplished jazz musicians play in a swing style. CD Tracks 19-26 provide some examples.

▶ IMPROVISATION STUDY A is a D dorian (Concert C dorian) scale played in a swing style.
▶ Strive to match the phrasing and articulation of the trumpet, tenor sax, and trombone on the recording.

▶ These licks are derived from the D dorian (Concert C dorian) scale, and are played in a swing style.

You are now ready to solo on MINOR ATTITUDE. Use the SUGGESTED SOLO on page 13 as a starting point, or continue with the ADVANCED IMPROVISATION STUDIES.

ADVANCED IMPROVISATION STUDIES – MINOR ATTITUDE

MINOR SEVENTH CHORDS

In addition to scales and scale fragments, the use of chord tones is common when improvising. In MINOR ATTITUDE, use Dmi7 and Emi7 chord tones as indicated by the chord symbols.

C1 (LISTEN 1ST TIME, PLAY 2ND TIME) ◉22

DORIAN SCALES

Improvisers often change scales as the chords change. In MINOR ATTITUDE, use D dorian over Dmi7 and E dorian over Emi7.

C2 (LISTEN 1ST TIME, PLAY 2ND TIME) ◉23

C3 CALL AND RESPONSE ◉24

▶ In the bars with slashes, use swing rhythms combined with chord and scale tones from ADVANCED IMPROVISATION STUDIES C1 and C2 to create responses to the calls the first time. The second time, improvise the entire chorus.

C4 EAR OPENERS ◉25

▶ Listen to each lick, then echo it on your instrument.
▶ The first pitch shown is your starting pitch for the first two licks. The second pitch is your starting pitch for the third and fourth licks. Let your ears determine the starting pitches for the remaining licks.

When soloing on MINOR ATTITUDE, use the SUGGESTED SOLO on page 13 as a model.
For additional improvisation practice, use the SUGGESTED SOLO as an IMPROVISATION STUDY.

W35TP2

Minor Attitude

SUGGESTED SOLO – MINOR ATTITUDE

The SUGGESTED SOLO is intended as a model. Once you learn it, you may choose to perform it as written during the MINOR ATTITUDE solo section (bars 55-70). You are encouraged, however, to improvise a solo, even if your improvisation is largely based on the SUGGESTED SOLO.

To use the SUGGESTED SOLO as an IMPROVISATION STUDY with the CD, listen to the solo the first time, play the solo the second time, and improvise the third and fourth times.

▶ The SUGGESTED SOLO is constructed of licks derived from D and E DORIAN (Concert C and D dorian) scales, and Dmi7 and Emi7 (Concert Cmi7 and Dmi7) CHORD TONES. A lick from IMPROV STUDY B (IMPROVISATION STUDY B) is also included.
▶ If you bypassed the ADVANCED IMPROVISATION STUDIES on page 11, you may be unfamiliar with some of the chords and scales used in this solo. Review the ADVANCED IMPROVISATION STUDIES to learn more about these musical elements, or simply use the solo's pitches, rhythms, and licks as a starting point for your own improvisation.

IMPROVISATION STUDY – PRETTY EYES

PRETTY EYES is a **jazz ballad**. Jazz ballads are slow, relaxed compositions. Eighth notes are usually played straight, but the rhythm section groove retains many swing elements. Jazz ballads often have interesting, complex chord progressions.

To improvise over a ballad, jazz musicians often play an **embellished** version of the melody as their solo. While melodic embellishment often retains the shape and character of the melody, the soloist may add or delete some notes, or alter rhythms slightly.

Rhythm section with original melody (bars 36-52)  27

Rhythm section with embellished melody (bars 36-52)  28

Rhythm section only (bars 36-52)  29

▶ Use the SOLO PART when practicing with the CD or when performing as a soloist with a jazz ensemble.
▶ Listen to Tracks 27 and 28, then play bars 36-52 of the SOLO PART with the rhythm section accompaniment on Track 29.
Try playing the original melody as written, the embellished melody as written, and your own embellished version of the melody.
▶ Use the JAZZ ENSEMBLE PART when you are playing in your section and are not playing the solo.

PRETTY EYES
(SOLO PART)

Pretty Eyes
(Jazz Ensemble Part)

Jazz Ballad ♩ = 66-72

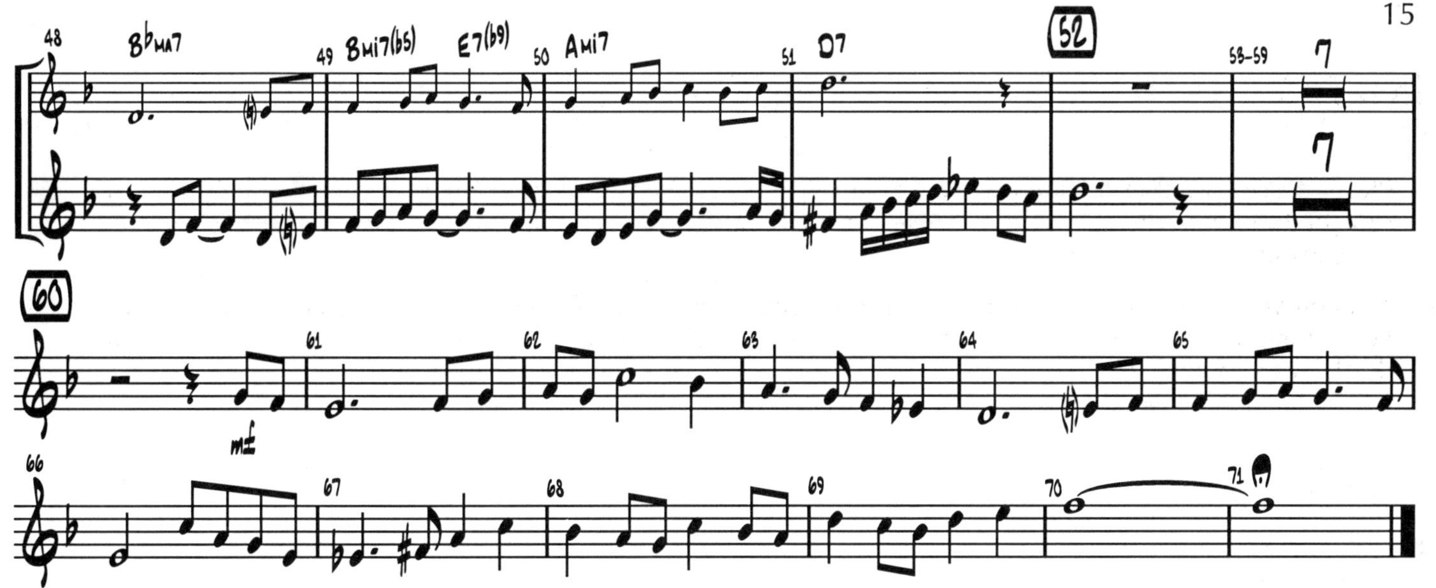

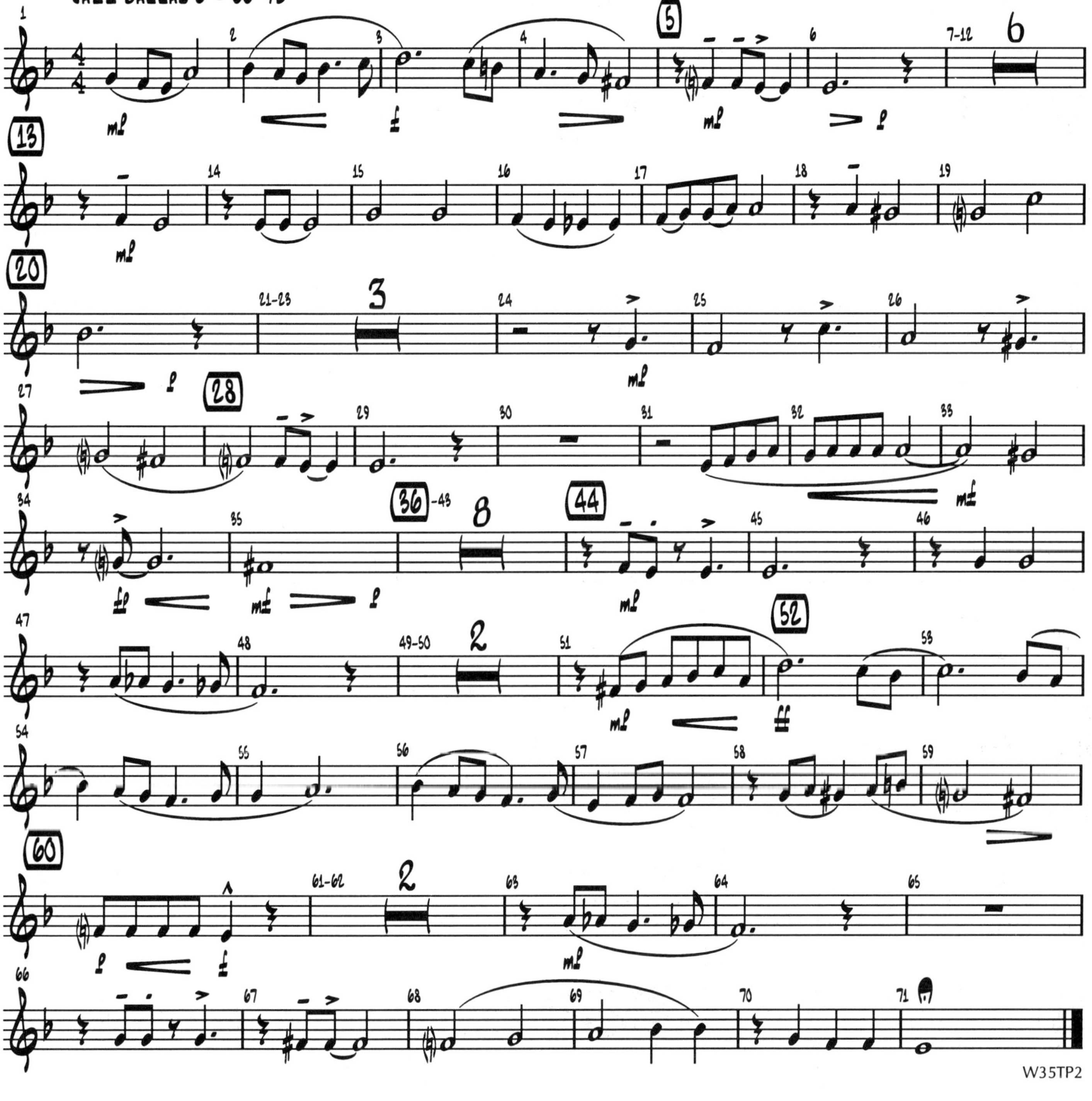

Performance Study – The Check's in the Mail

SWING

THE CHECK'S IN THE MAIL is an **up swing** (fast swing) sax section feature. Playing at a fast tempo requires strong technical **chops** on your instrument, and a solid sense of **time** throughout the ensemble.

It is critical that you always listen carefully as you play to ensure that your phrasing and articulation match the other members of the ensemble.

A Up Swing ♩ = 176–192

Saxophone, Trumpet, and Trombone with rhythm section (no Drums) 30

Rhythm section only 31

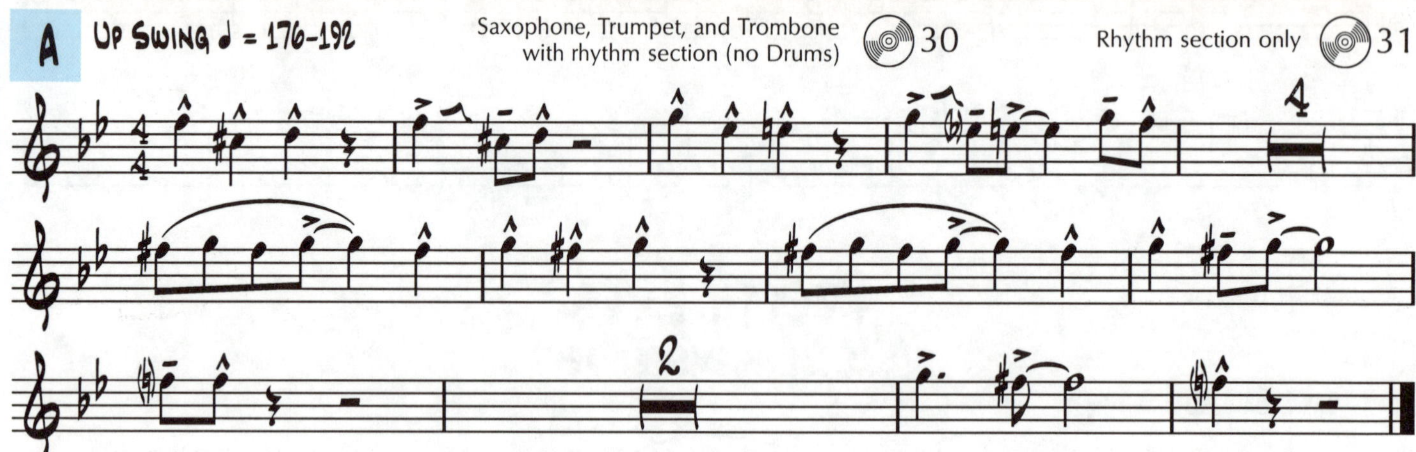

- CD Track 30 provides a model of how this PERFORMANCE STUDY should sound. Listen carefully to the phrasing and articulation used by the alto sax, trumpet, and trombone on the recording. Imagine that these are the **lead** players in your jazz ensemble. (Track 30 is also a play-along track for drums, so only the drummer's hi-hat is heard.)
- After listening to Track 30, practice this study at a slow tempo using a metronome. Once mastered, practice at full tempo with Track 31. You may also practice with Track 30 to develop your section-playing skills.

The Check's in the Mail

Up Swing ♩ = 176–192

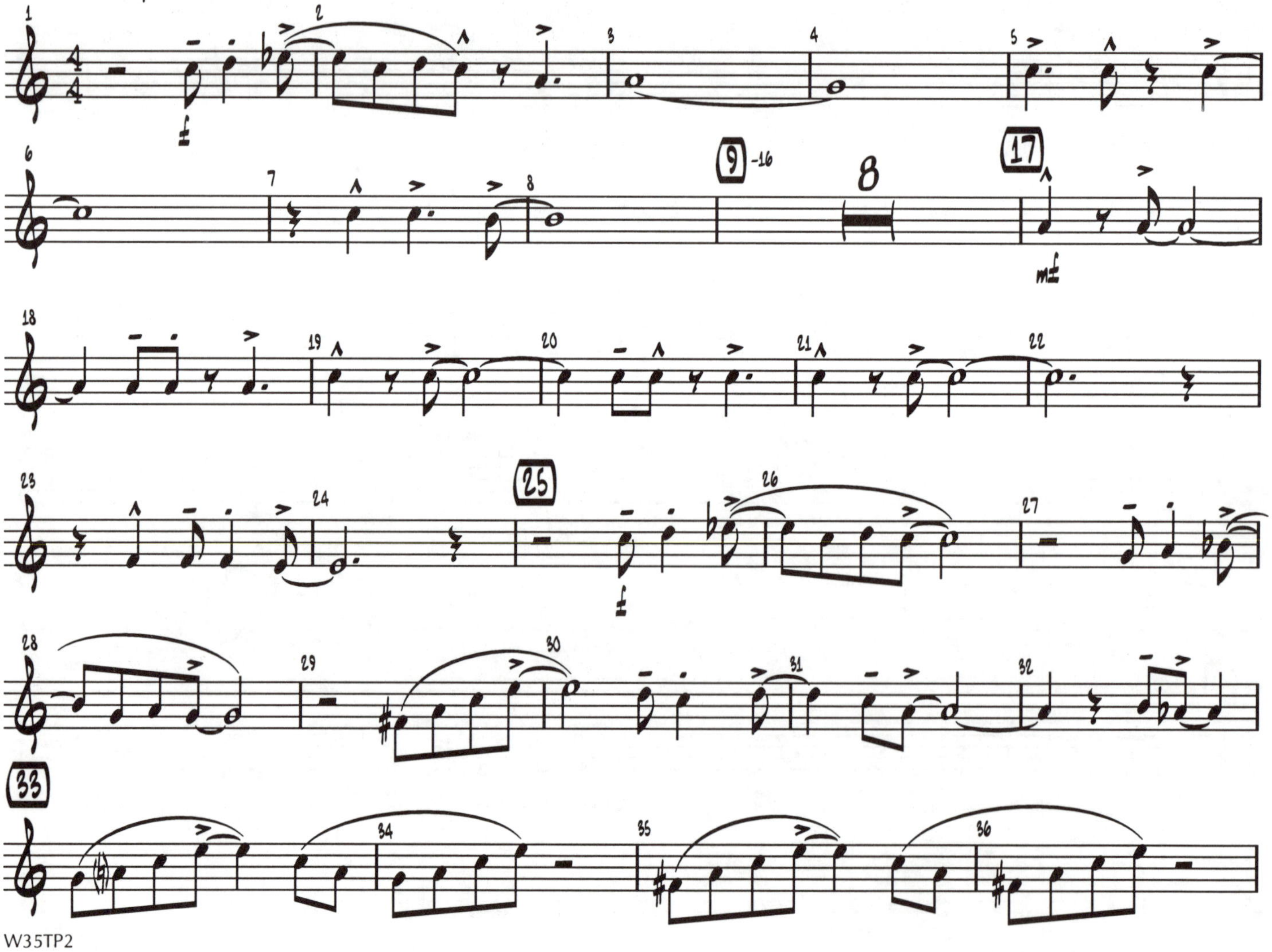

Sax Soli Break

IMPROVISATION STUDIES – COCO LOCO

DORIAN SCALE

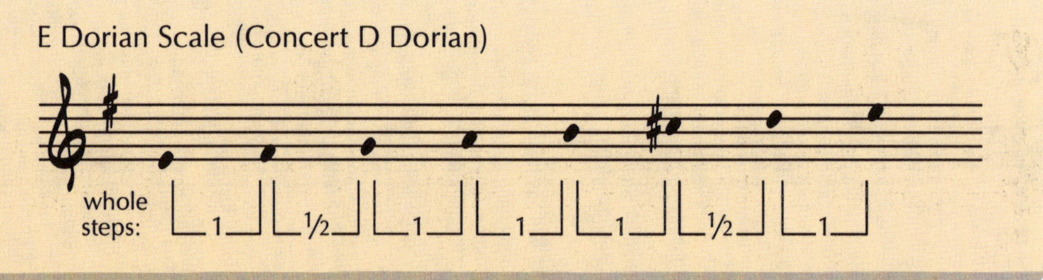

The dorian scale is a common choice when improvising over a minor seventh chord, like Emi7 (Concert Dmi7) in the COCO LOCO solo section. The solo section requires the use of the E dorian (Concert D dorian) scale only, even though the chords alternate between a minor seventh chord and a dominant seventh chord: Emi7 to A7 (Concert Dmi7 to G7).

COCO LOCO is a **bossa nova** (or **bossa**). When improvising, choose rhythms in that same style for your solos. Develop the necessary rhythm vocabulary by listening to accomplished jazz musicians play in a bossa style. CD Tracks 32-39 provide some examples.

Bossa ♩ = 132-144

▶ IMPROVISATION STUDY A is an E dorian (Concert D dorian) scale played in a bossa style.
▶ Strive to match the phrasing and articulation of the trumpet, tenor sax, and trombone on the recording.

▶ These licks are derived from the E dorian (Concert D dorian) scale, and are played in a bossa style.
▶ Listen carefully to the tenor sax on the recording. Be sure to match the player's phrasing and articulation.

IMPROVISATION STUDIES – COCO LOCO, cont.

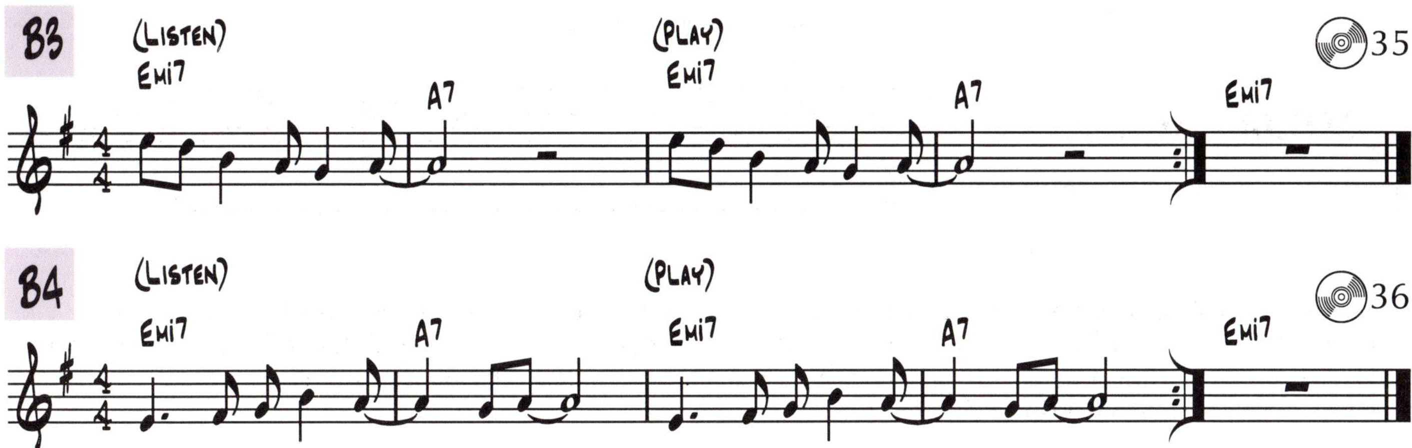

▶ These licks are derived from the E dorian (Concert D dorian) scale, and are played in a bossa style.

You are now ready to solo on COCO LOCO. Use the SUGGESTED SOLO on page 21 as a starting point, or continue with the ADVANCED IMPROVISATION STUDIES.

ADVANCED IMPROVISATION STUDIES – COCO LOCO

Call and response is a performance style in which musicians carry on a back-and-forth musical dialogue. The call is a musical statement or question, and the response provides a musical answer.

C1 CALL AND RESPONSE

▶ In the bars with slashes, use bossa rhythms combined with pitches from the E dorian scale to create responses to the calls the first time. The second time, improvise the entire chorus.

C2 EAR OPENERS

▶ Listen to each lick, then echo it on your instrument. As you play, echo not only the pitches and rhythms, but also the phrasing and articulation exactly as you hear them.
▶ The pitch shown is your starting pitch for all of the licks in this exercise.

When soloing on COCO LOCO, use the SUGGESTED SOLO on page 21 as a model. For additional improvisation practice, use the SUGGESTED SOLO as an IMPROVISATION STUDY.

Coco Loco

▶ At the **solo break** in bar 56, everyone except the first soloist rests. During this break, the soloist should improvise a lead-in to his or her solo using notes from the E dorian (Concert D dorian) scale.

SUGGESTED SOLO – COCO LOCO

The SUGGESTED SOLO is intended as a model. Once you learn it, you may choose to perform it as written during the COCO LOCO solo section (bars 57-64). You are encouraged, however, to improvise a solo, even if your improvisation is largely based on the SUGGESTED SOLO.

To use the SUGGESTED SOLO as an IMPROVISATION STUDY with the CD, listen to the solo the first time, play the solo the second time, and improvise the third and fourth times.

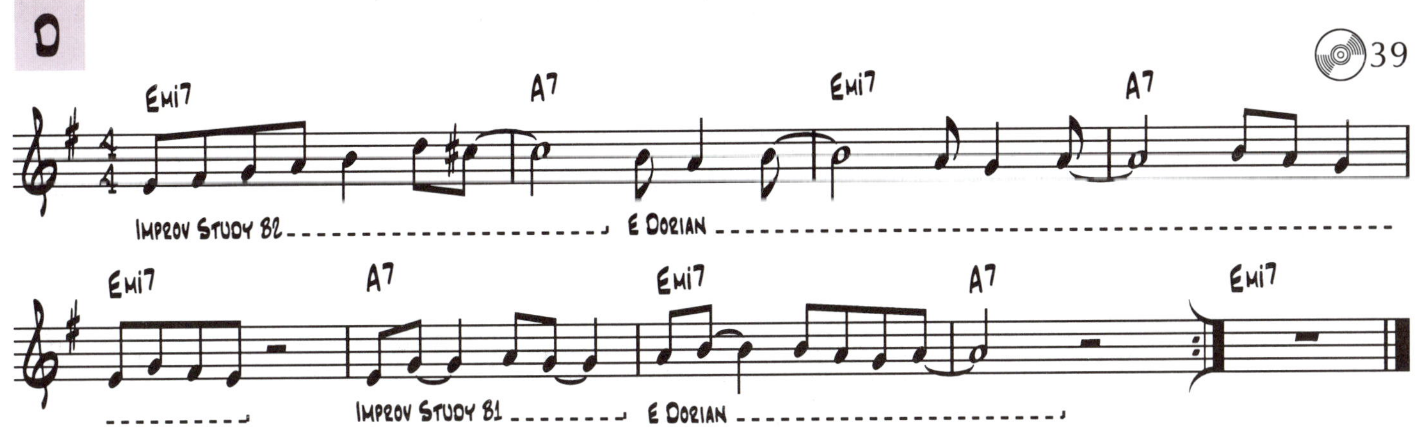

▶ The SUGGESTED SOLO is constructed of licks derived from the **E DORIAN** (Concert D dorian) scale. Licks from **IMPROV STUDY B** (IMPROVISATION STUDY B) are also included.

IMPROVISATION STUDIES – SUMMER HEAT

NATURAL MINOR SCALE

The **natural minor scale**, also known as the **aeolian scale**, is a possible choice when improvising over a minor seventh chord, like Ami7 (Concert Gmi7) in the SUMMER HEAT solo section. The solo section requires the use of the A natural minor (Concert G natural minor) scale only, even though the chords alternate between a minor seventh chord and a dominant seventh chord: Ami7 to G7 (Concert Gmi7 to F7).

SUMMER HEAT is a **samba**. When improvising, choose rhythms in that same style for your solos. Develop the necessary rhythm vocabulary by listening to accomplished jazz musicians play in a samba style. CD Tracks 40-47 provide some examples.

SAMBA ♩ = 160–172

▶ IMPROVISATION STUDY A is an A natural minor (Concert G natural minor) scale played in a samba style.
▶ Strive to match the phrasing and articulation of the trumpet, tenor sax, and trombone on the recording.

▶ These licks are derived from the A natural minor (Concert G natural minor) scale, and are played in a samba style.

You are now ready to solo on SUMMER HEAT. Use the SUGGESTED SOLO on page 25 as a starting point, or continue with the ADVANCED IMPROVISATION STUDIES.

ADVANCED IMPROVISATION STUDIES – SUMMER HEAT

MINOR SEVENTH & DOMINANT SEVENTH CHORDS

In SUMMER HEAT, use Ami7 and G7 chord tones as indicated by the chord symbols above the music.

C1 (LISTEN 1ST TIME, PLAY 2ND TIME) — 43

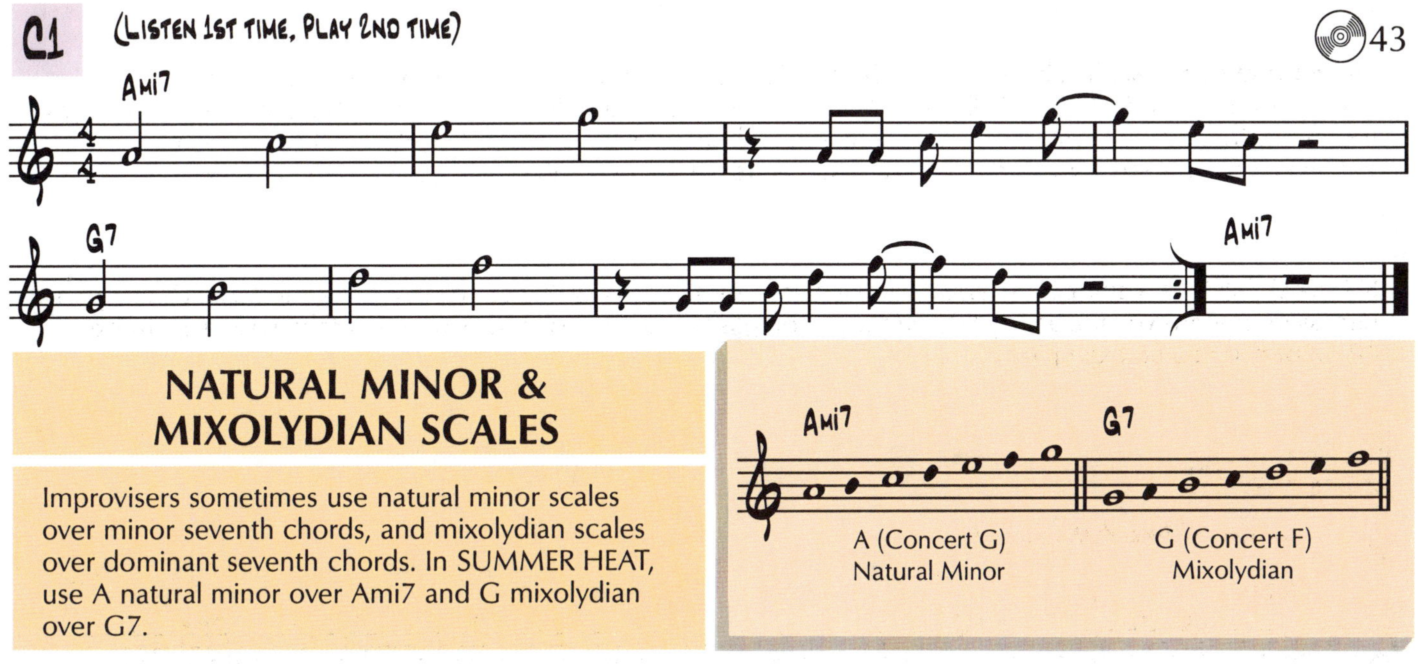

NATURAL MINOR & MIXOLYDIAN SCALES

Improvisers sometimes use natural minor scales over minor seventh chords, and mixolydian scales over dominant seventh chords. In SUMMER HEAT, use A natural minor over Ami7 and G mixolydian over G7.

C2 (LISTEN 1ST TIME, PLAY 2ND TIME) — 44

C3 CALL AND RESPONSE — 45

▶ In the bars with slashes, use samba rhythms combined with chord and scale tones from ADVANCED IMPROVISATION STUDIES C1 and C2 to create responses to the calls the first time. The second time, improvise the entire chorus.

C4 EAR OPENERS — 46

▶ Listen to each lick, then echo it on your instrument.
▶ The first pitch shown is your starting pitch for the first two licks. The second pitch is your starting pitch for the third and fourth licks. Let your ears determine the starting pitches for the remaining licks.

When soloing on SUMMER HEAT, use the SUGGESTED SOLO on page 25 as a model.
For additional improvisation practice, use the SUGGESTED SOLO as an IMPROVISATION STUDY.

Summer Heat

▶ At the solo break in bar 52, everyone except the first soloist rests. During this break, the soloist should improvise a lead-in to his or her solo using notes from the A natural minor (Concert G natural minor) scale.

W35TP2

SUGGESTED SOLO – SUMMER HEAT

The SUGGESTED SOLO is intended as a model. Once you learn it, you may choose to perform it as written during the SUMMER HEAT solo section (bars 53-68). You are encouraged, however, to improvise a solo, even if your improvisation is largely based on the SUGGESTED SOLO.

To use the SUGGESTED SOLO as an IMPROVISATION STUDY with the CD, listen to the solo the first time, play the solo the second time, and improvise the third and fourth times.

► The SUGGESTED SOLO is constructed of licks derived from **A NATURAL MINOR** and **G MIXOLYDIAN** (Concert G natural minor and F mixolydian) scales, and Ami7 and G7 (Concert Gmi7 and F7) **CHORD TONES**. A lick from **IMPROV STUDY B** (IMPROVISATION STUDY B) is also included.

► If you bypassed the ADVANCED IMPROVISATION STUDIES on page 23, you may be unfamiliar with some of the chords and scales used in this solo. Review the ADVANCED IMPROVISATION STUDIES to learn more about these musical elements, or simply use the solo's pitches, rhythms, and licks as a starting point for your own improvisation.

IMPROVISATION STUDIES – SAN JUAN BY NIGHT

DORIAN SCALE

The dorian scale is a common choice when improvising over a minor seventh chord, like Ami7 (Concert Gmi7) in the SAN JUAN BY NIGHT solo section. The solo section requires the use of the A dorian (Concert G dorian) scale only, even though the chords alternate between a minor seventh chord and a dominant seventh chord: Ami7 to D7 (Concert Gmi7 to C7).

SAN JUAN BY NIGHT is a **salsa** tune. When improvising, choose rhythms in that same style for your solos. Develop the necessary rhythm vocabulary by listening to accomplished jazz musicians play in a salsa style. CD Tracks 48-55 provide some examples.

SALSA ♩ = 160-172

A (LISTEN 1ST TIME, PLAY 2ND TIME) 48

▶ IMPROVISATION STUDY A is an A dorian (Concert G dorian) scale played in a salsa style.
▶ Strive to match the phrasing and articulation of the trumpet, tenor sax, and trombone on the recording.

B1 (LISTEN)   (PLAY) 49

B2 (LISTEN)   (PLAY) 50

▶ These licks are derived from the A dorian (Concert G dorian) scale, and are played in a salsa style.

You are now ready to solo on SAN JUAN BY NIGHT. Use the SUGGESTED SOLO on page 29 as a starting point, or continue with the ADVANCED IMPROVISATION STUDIES.

ADVANCED IMPROVISATION STUDIES – SAN JUAN BY NIGHT

MINOR SEVENTH & DOMINANT SEVENTH CHORDS

In SAN JUAN BY NIGHT, use Ami7 and D7 chord tones. This chord movement from minor seventh to dominant seventh a perfect fifth lower is called a ii7-V7 (or simply ii-V) progression.

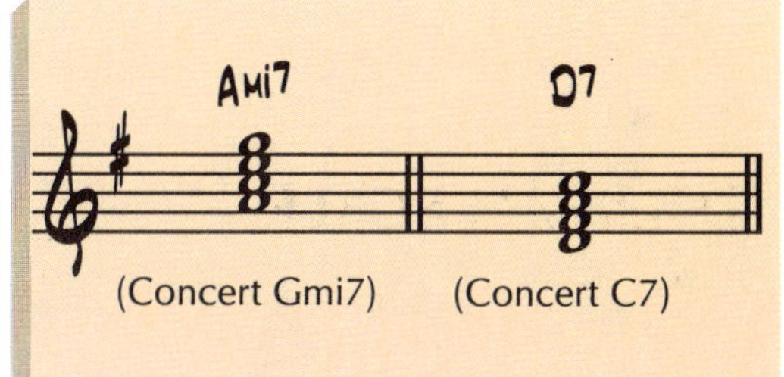

C1 (LISTEN 1ST TIME, PLAY 2ND TIME) 🔊51

DORIAN & MIXOLYDIAN SCALES

Improvisers commonly use dorian scales over minor seventh chords, and mixolydian scales over dominant seventh chords. In SAN JUAN BY NIGHT, use A dorian over Ami7 and D mixolydian over D7.

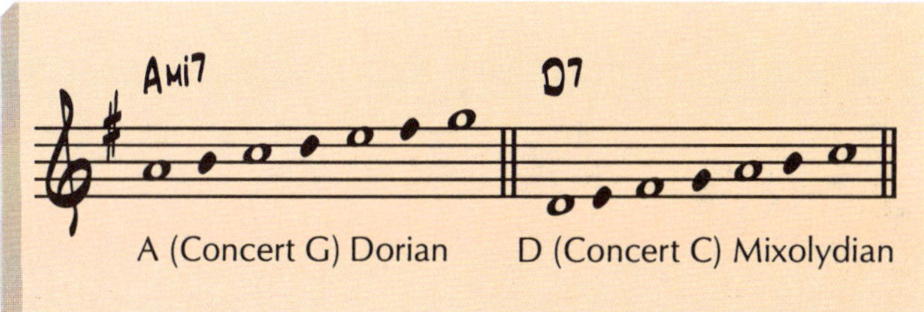

C2 (LISTEN 1ST TIME, PLAY 2ND TIME) 🔊52

C3 CALL AND RESPONSE 🔊53

▶ In the bars with slashes, use salsa rhythms combined with chord and scale tones from ADVANCED IMPROVISATION STUDIES C1 and C2 to create responses to the calls the first time. The second time, improvise the entire chorus.

C4 EAR OPENERS 🔊54

▶ Listen to each lick, then echo it on your instrument.
▶ The first pitch shown is your starting pitch for the first two licks. The second pitch is your starting pitch for the third and fourth licks. Let your ears determine the starting pitches for the remaining licks.

When soloing on SAN JUAN BY NIGHT, use the SUGGESTED SOLO on page 29 as a model.
For additional improvisation practice, use the SUGGESTED SOLO as an IMPROVISATION STUDY.

San Juan by Night

SUGGESTED SOLO – SAN JUAN BY NIGHT

The SUGGESTED SOLO is intended as a model. Once you learn it, you may choose to perform it as written during the SAN JUAN BY NIGHT solo section (bars 53-68). You are encouraged, however, to improvise a solo, even if your improvisation is largely based on the SUGGESTED SOLO.

To use the SUGGESTED SOLO as an IMPROVISATION STUDY with the CD, listen to the solo the first time, play the solo the second time, and improvise the third and fourth times.

▶ The SUGGESTED SOLO is constructed of licks derived from **A Dorian** and **D Mixolydian** (Concert G dorian and C mixolydian) scales, and Ami7 and D7 (Concert Gmi7 and C7) **Chord Tones**. Licks from **Improv Study B** (IMPROVISATION STUDY B) are also included.

▶ If you bypassed the ADVANCED IMPROVISATION STUDIES on page 27, you may be unfamiliar with some of the chords and scales used in this solo. Review the ADVANCED IMPROVISATION STUDIES to learn more about these musical elements, or simply use the solo's pitches, rhythms, and licks as a starting point for your own improvisation.

IMPROVISATION STUDIES – MUTUAL DECEPTION

BLUES SCALE

While MUTUAL DECEPTION is based on the dorian scale, the solo section is a minor blues progression. Like a standard blues, the progression is twelve bars long, but uses minor seventh chords instead of dominant seventh chords. In spite of these differences, the blues scale can still be used when soloing. Since the tonic note of the solo section is G (Concert F), use a G blues (Concert F blues) scale.

MUTUAL DECEPTION is an **Afro-Cuban** tune. When improvising, choose rhythms in that same style for your solos. Develop the necessary rhythm vocabulary by listening to accomplished jazz musicians play in an Afro-Cuban style. CD Tracks 56-63 provide some examples.

▶ IMPROVISATION STUDY A is a G blues (Concert F blues) scale played in an Afro-Cuban style.
▶ Strive to match the phrasing and articulation of the trumpet, tenor sax, and trombone on the recording.

▶ These licks are derived from the G blues (Concert F blues) scale, and are played in an Afro-Cuban style.

You are now ready to solo on MUTUAL DECEPTION. Use the SUGGESTED SOLO on page 33 as a starting point, or continue with the ADVANCED IMPROVISATION STUDIES.

ADVANCED IMPROVISATION STUDIES – MUTUAL DECEPTION

MINOR SEVENTH CHORDS

In MUTUAL DECEPTION, use Gmi7 and Cmi7 chord tones as indicated by the chord symbols above the music.

C1 (LISTEN 1ST TIME, PLAY 2ND TIME) — 59

DORIAN SCALES

While blues scale fragments work well when improvising over the minor seventh chords in MUTUAL DECEPTION, improvisers may also use dorian scales. Use G dorian over Gmi7 and C dorian over Cmi7.

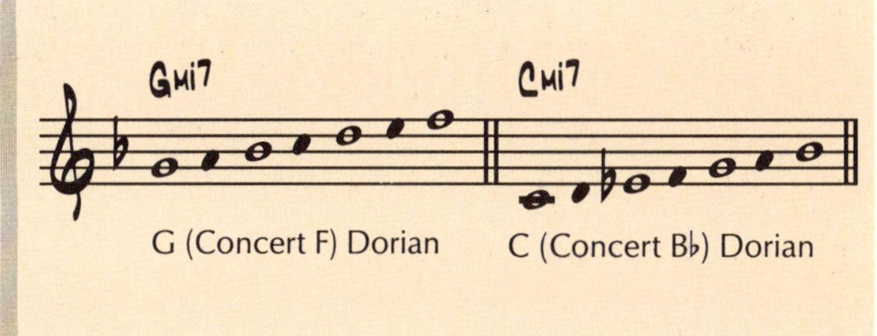

C2 (LISTEN 1ST TIME, PLAY 2ND TIME) — 60

C3 CALL AND RESPONSE — 61

► In the bars with slashes, use Afro-Cuban rhythms combined with chord and scale tones from ADVANCED IMPROVISATION STUDIES C1 and C2 to create responses to the calls the first time. The second time, improvise the entire chorus.

C4 EAR OPENERS — 62

► Listen to each lick, then echo it on your instrument.
► The first pitch shown is your starting pitch for the first two licks. The second pitch is your starting pitch for the third and fourth licks. Let your ears determine the starting pitches for the remaining licks.

When soloing on MUTUAL DECEPTION, use the SUGGESTED SOLO on page 33 as a model. For additional improvisation practice, use the SUGGESTED SOLO as an IMPROVISATION STUDY.

Mutual Deception

SUGGESTED SOLO – MUTUAL DECEPTION

The SUGGESTED SOLO is intended as a model. Once you learn it, you may choose to perform it as written during the MUTUAL DECEPTION solo section (bars 38-49). You are encouraged, however, to improvise a solo, even if your improvisation is largely based on the SUGGESTED SOLO.

To use the SUGGESTED SOLO as an IMPROVISATION STUDY with the CD, listen to the solo the first time, play the solo the second time, and improvise the third and fourth times.

▶ The SUGGESTED SOLO is constructed of licks derived from **G BLUES** and **C DORIAN** (Concert F blues and B♭ dorian) scales, and Gmi7 and Cmi7 (Concert Fmi7 and B♭mi7) **CHORD TONES**.

▶ If you bypassed the ADVANCED IMPROVISATION STUDIES on page 31, you may be unfamiliar with some of the chords and scales used in this solo. Review the ADVANCED IMPROVISATION STUDIES to learn more about these musical elements, or simply use the solo's pitches, rhythms, and licks as a starting point for your own improvisation.

Improvisation Studies – Go Charlie, Go!

MIXOLYDIAN SCALE

The mixolydian scale may be used when soloing over GO CHARLIE, GO! The mixolydian scale is a common choice when improvising over a dominant seventh chord, like G7 (Concert F7) in the GO CHARLIE, GO! solo section.

GO CHARLIE, GO! is a **rock** tune. When improvising, choose rhythms in that same style for your solos. Develop the necessary rhythm vocabulary by listening to accomplished jazz musicians play in a rock style. CD Tracks 64-71 provide some examples.

Rock ♩ = 138–152

A (Listen 1st time, Play 2nd time) 64

- IMPROVISATION STUDY A is a G mixolydian (Concert F mixolydian) scale played in a rock style.
- Strive to match the phrasing and articulation of the trumpet, tenor sax, and trombone on the recording.
- The D7sus (Concert C7sus) chord is used to mark the end of each eight bar solo chorus, and lead, or **turnaround**, to the beginning of the next chorus. Continue to use the G mixolydian (Concert F mixolydian) scale when improvising over this chord.

B1 (Listen) (Play) 65

B2 (Listen) (Play) 66

- These licks are derived from the G mixolydian (Concert F mixolydian) scale, and are played in a rock style.
- Listen carefully to the trumpet on the recording. Be sure to match the player's phrasing and articulation.

IMPROVISATION STUDIES – GO CHARLIE, GO!, cont.

▶ These licks are derived from the G mixolydian (Concert F mixolydian) scale, and are played in a rock style.

You are now ready to solo on GO CHARLIE, GO! Use the SUGGESTED SOLO on page 37 as a starting point, or continue with the ADVANCED IMPROVISATION STUDIES.

ADVANCED IMPROVISATION STUDIES – GO CHARLIE, GO!

Call and response is a performance style in which musicians carry on a back-and-forth musical dialogue. The call is a musical statement or question, and the response provides a musical answer.

C1 CALL AND RESPONSE

▶ In the bars with slashes, use rock rhythms combined with pitches from the G mixolydian scale to create responses to the calls the first time. The second time, improvise the entire chorus.
▶ When improvising over the D7sus chord, continue to use the G mixolydian scale.

C2 EAR OPENERS

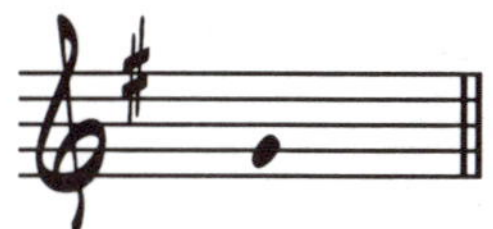

▶ Listen to each lick, then echo it on your instrument. As you play, echo not only the pitches and rhythms, but also the phrasing and articulation exactly as you hear them.
▶ The pitch shown is your starting pitch for all of the licks in this exercise.

When soloing on GO CHARLIE, GO!, use the SUGGESTED SOLO on page 37 as a model.
For additional improvisation practice, use the SUGGESTED SOLO as an IMPROVISATION STUDY.

Go Charlie, Go!

SUGGESTED SOLO – GO CHARLIE, GO!

The SUGGESTED SOLO is intended as a model. Once you learn it, you may choose to perform it as written during the GO CHARLIE, GO! solo section (bars 43-50). You are encouraged, however, to improvise a solo, even if your improvisation is largely based on the SUGGESTED SOLO.

To use the SUGGESTED SOLO as an IMPROVISATION STUDY with the CD, listen to the solo the first time, play the solo the second time, and improvise the third and fourth times.

▶ The SUGGESTED SOLO is constructed of licks derived from the **G MIXOLYDIAN** (Concert F mixolydian) scale. Licks from **IMPROV STUDY B** (IMPROVISATION STUDY B) are also included.

▶ When improvising over the the D7sus chord, continue to use the G mixolydian scale.

IMPROVISATION STUDIES – WHERE YOU WANT TO BE

DORIAN SCALE

The dorian scale is a common choice when improvising over a minor seventh chord, like Ami7 (Concert Gmi7) in the WHERE YOU WANT TO BE solo section. The solo section requires the use of the A dorian (Concert G dorian) scale only, even though the chords alternate between a minor seventh chord and a dominant seventh chord: Ami7 to D7 (Concert Gmi7 to C7).

WHERE YOU WANT TO BE is a **funk** tune. When improvising, choose rhythms in that same style for your solos. Develop the necessary rhythm vocabulary by listening to accomplished jazz musicians play in a funk style. CD Tracks 72-79 provide some examples.

FUNK ♩ = 92–100

▶ IMPROVISATION STUDY A is an A dorian (Concert G dorian) scale played in a funk style.
▶ Strive to match the phrasing and articulation of the trumpet, tenor sax, and trombone on the recording.

▶ These licks are derived from the A dorian (Concert G dorian) scale, and are played in a funk style.

You are now ready to solo on WHERE YOU WANT TO BE. Use the SUGGESTED SOLO on page 41 as a starting point, or continue with the ADVANCED IMPROVISATION STUDIES.

ADVANCED IMPROVISATION STUDIES – WHERE YOU WANT TO BE

MINOR SEVENTH & DOMINANT SEVENTH CHORDS

In WHERE YOU WANT TO BE, use Ami7 and D7 chord tones. This chord movement from minor seventh to dominant seventh a perfect fifth lower is called a ii7-V7 (or simply ii-V) progression.

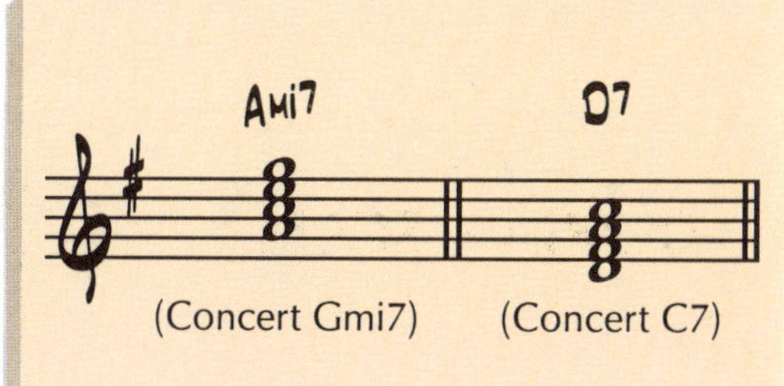

C1 (LISTEN 1ST TIME, PLAY 2ND TIME) 75

DORIAN & MIXOLYDIAN SCALES

Improvisers commonly use dorian scales over minor seventh chords, and mixolydian scales over dominant seventh chords. In WHERE YOU WANT TO BE, use A dorian over Ami7 and D mixolydian over D7.

C2 (LISTEN 1ST TIME, PLAY 2ND TIME) 76

C3 CALL AND RESPONSE 77

▶ In the bars with slashes, use funk rhythms combined with chord and scale tones from ADVANCED IMPROVISATION STUDIES C1 and C2 to create responses to the calls the first time. The second time, improvise the entire chorus.

C4 EAR OPENERS 78

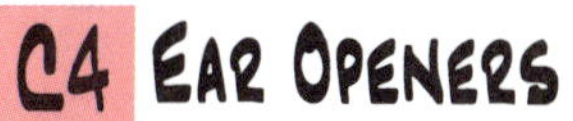

▶ Listen to each lick, then echo it on your instrument.
▶ The first pitch shown is your starting pitch for the first two licks. The second pitch is your starting pitch for the third and fourth licks. Let your ears determine the starting pitches for the remaining licks.

When soloing on WHERE YOU WANT TO BE, use the SUGGESTED SOLO on page 41 as a model. For additional improvisation practice, use the SUGGESTED SOLO as an IMPROVISATION STUDY.

W35TP2

Where You Want to Be

SUGGESTED SOLO – WHERE YOU WANT TO BE

The SUGGESTED SOLO is intended as a model. Once you learn it, you may choose to perform it as written during the WHERE YOU WANT TO BE solo section (bars 33-48). You are encouraged, however, to improvise a solo, even if your improvisation is largely based on the SUGGESTED SOLO.

To use the SUGGESTED SOLO as an IMPROVISATION STUDY with the CD, listen to the solo the first time, play the solo the second time, and improvise the third and fourth times.

▶ The SUGGESTED SOLO is constructed of licks derived from **A Dorian** and **D Mixolydian** (Concert G dorian and C mixolydian) scales, and Ami7 and D7 (Concert Gmi7 and C7) **Chord Tones**. A lick from **Improv Study B** (IMPROVISATION STUDY B) is also included.

▶ If you bypassed the ADVANCED IMPROVISATION STUDIES on page 39, you may be unfamiliar with some of the chords and scales used in this solo. Review the ADVANCED IMPROVISATION STUDIES to learn more about these musical elements, or simply use the solo's pitches, rhythms, and licks as a starting point for your own improvisation.

IMPROVISATION STUDY - LITTLEST ONE

LITTLEST ONE is a **rock ballad**. Rock ballads are slow compositions, usually in $\frac{4}{4}$, with a steady eighth note or sixteenth note groove. They often have interesting, complex chord progressions.

To improvise over a ballad, jazz musicians often play an embellished version of the melody as their solo. While melodic embellishment often retains the shape and character of the melody, the soloist may add or delete some notes, or alter rhythms slightly.

Rhythm section with original melody (bars 29-44)  80

Rhythm section with embellished melody (bars 29-44)  81

Rhythm section only (bars 29-44)  82

▶ Use the SOLO PART when practicing with the CD or when performing as a soloist with a jazz ensemble.
▶ Listen to Tracks 80 and 81, then play bars 29-44 of the SOLO PART with the rhythm section accompaniment on Track 82.
Try playing the original melody as written, the embellished melody as written, and your own embellished version of the melody.
▶ Use the JAZZ ENSEMBLE PART when you are playing in your section and are not playing the solo.

LITTLEST ONE
(SOLO PART)

LITTLEST ONE
(JAZZ ENSEMBLE PART)

IMPROVISATION STUDIES – ROCK THE HOUSE

NATURAL MINOR SCALE

The natural minor scale is a possible choice when improvising over a minor seventh chord, like Emi7 (Concert Dmi7) in the ROCK THE HOUSE solo section. The solo section requires the use of the E natural minor (Concert D natural minor) scale only, even though the chords alternate between a minor seventh chord and a **major seventh chord**: Emi7 to CMA7 (Concert Dmi7 to B♭MA7).

ROCK THE HOUSE is a **funk-shuffle** tune. When improvising, choose rhythms in that same style for your solos. Develop the necessary rhythm vocabulary by listening to accomplished jazz musicians play in a funk-shuffle style. CD Tracks 83-90 provide some examples.

FUNK SHUFFLE ♩ = 80-88
(SWING EIGHTHS)

▶ IMPROVISATION STUDY A is an E natural minor (Concert D natural minor) scale played in a funk-shuffle style.
▶ Strive to match the phrasing and articulation of the trumpet, tenor sax, and trombone on the recording.

▶ These licks are derived from the E natural minor (Concert D natural minor) scale, and are played in a funk-shuffle style.

You are now ready to solo on ROCK THE HOUSE. Use the SUGGESTED SOLO on page 47 as a starting point, or continue with the ADVANCED IMPROVISATION STUDIES.

ADVANCED IMPROVISATION STUDIES – ROCK THE HOUSE

MINOR SEVENTH & MAJOR SEVENTH CHORDS

In ROCK THE HOUSE, use Emi7 and CMA7 chord tones as indicated by the chord symbols above the music.

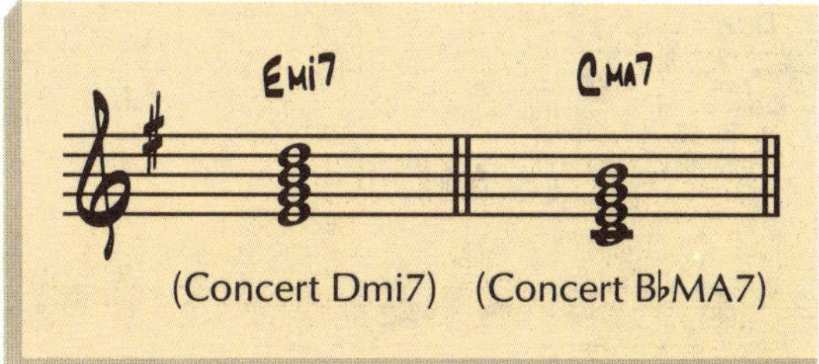

C1 (LISTEN 1ST TIME, PLAY 2ND TIME) 86

NATURAL MINOR & LYDIAN SCALES

Improvisers sometimes use natural minor scales over minor seventh chords and **lydian scales** over major seventh chords. In ROCK THE HOUSE, use E natural minor over Emi7 and C lydian over CMA7.

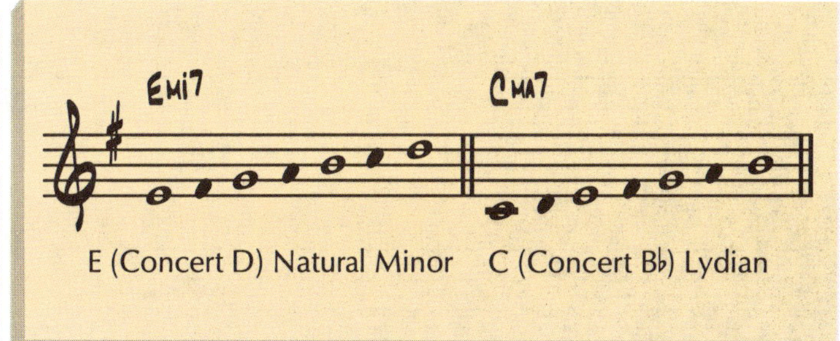

C2 (LISTEN 1ST TIME, PLAY 2ND TIME) 87

C3 CALL AND RESPONSE 88

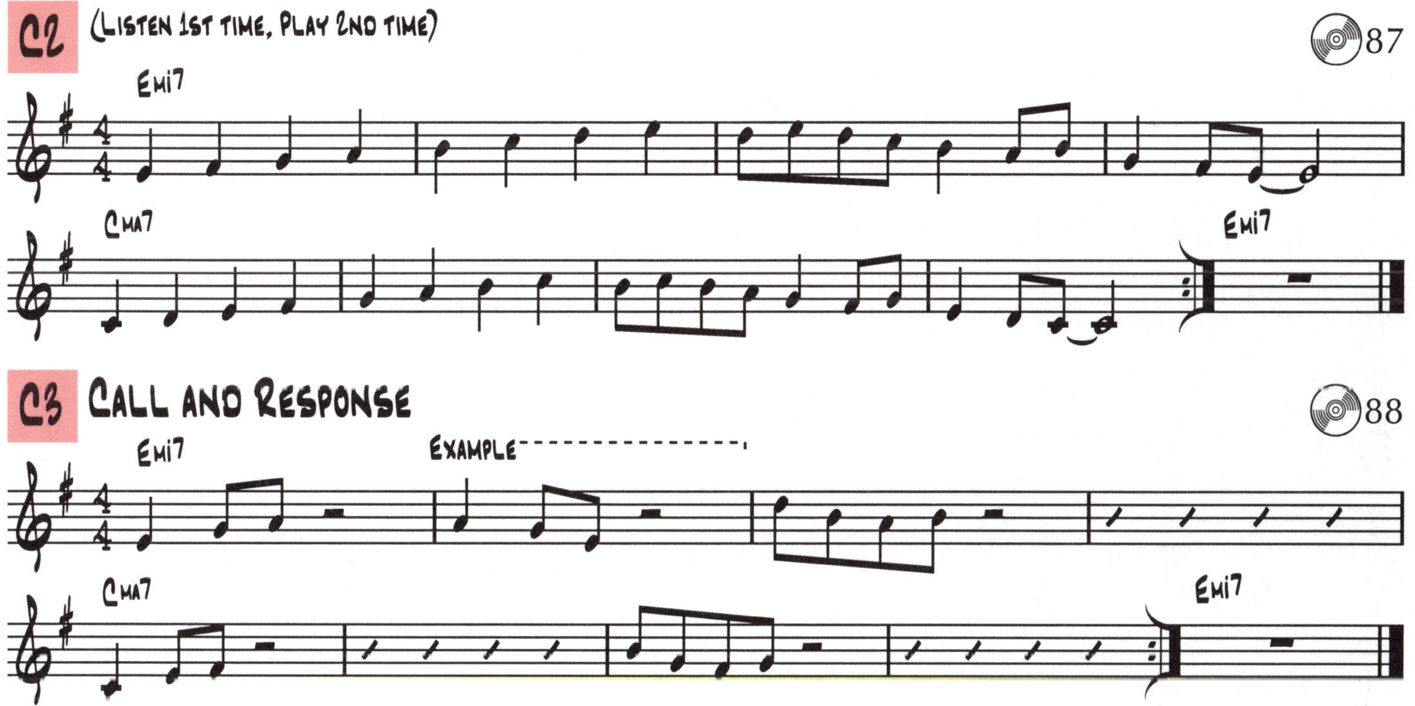

▶ In the bars with slashes, use funk-shuffle rhythms combined with chord and scale tones from ADVANCED IMPROVISATION STUDIES C1 and C2 to create responses to the calls the first time. The second time, improvise the entire chorus.

C4 EAR OPENERS 89

▶ Listen to each lick, then echo it on your instrument.
▶ The first pitch shown is your starting pitch for the first two licks. The second pitch is your starting pitch for the third and fourth licks. Let your ears determine the starting pitches for the remaining licks.

When soloing on ROCK THE HOUSE, use the SUGGESTED SOLO on page 47 as a model.
For additional improvisation practice, use the SUGGESTED SOLO as an IMPROVISATION STUDY.

Rock the House

▶ At the solo break in bar 54, everyone except the first soloist rests. During this break, the soloist should improvise a lead-in to his or her solo using notes from the E natural minor (Concert D natural minor) scale.

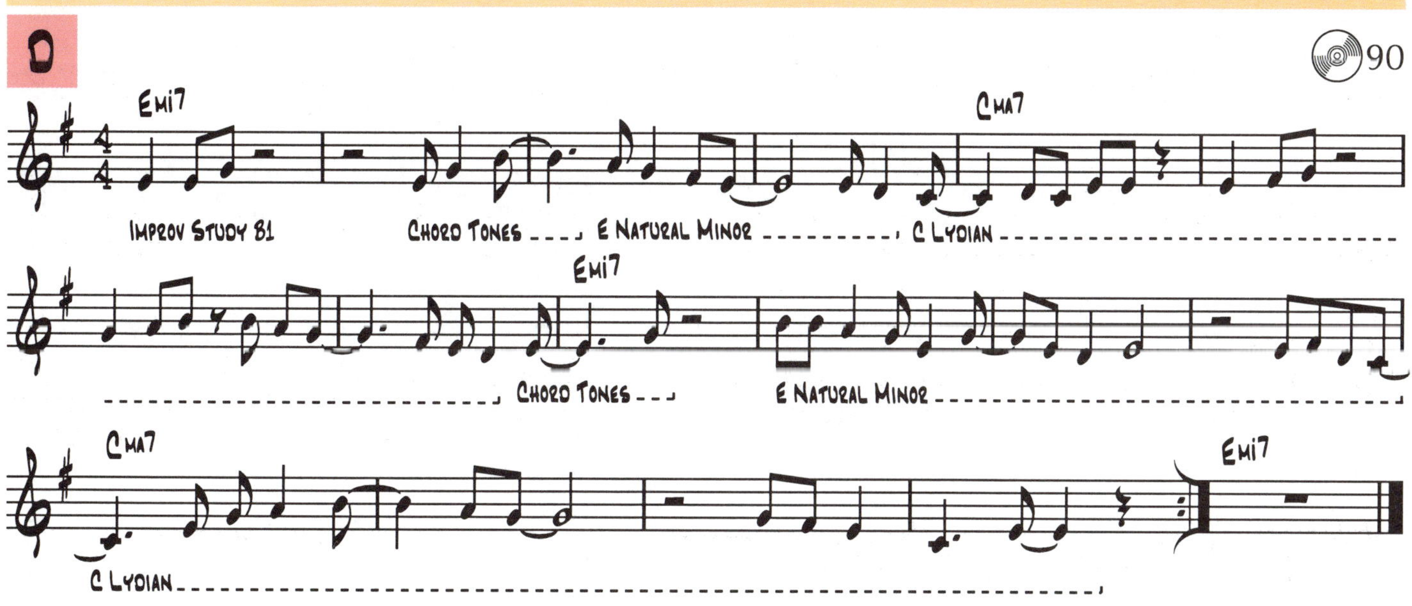

SUGGESTED SOLO - ROCK THE HOUSE

The SUGGESTED SOLO is intended as a model. Once you learn it, you may choose to perform it as written during the ROCK THE HOUSE solo section (bars 55-73). You are encouraged, however, to improvise a solo, even if your improvisation is largely based on the SUGGESTED SOLO.

To use the SUGGESTED SOLO as an IMPROVISATION STUDY with the CD, listen to the solo the first time, play the solo the second time, and improvise the third and fourth times.

▶ The SUGGESTED SOLO is constructed of licks derived from **E NATURAL MINOR** and **C LYDIAN** (Concert D natural minor and Bb lydian) scales, and Emi7 (Concert Dmi7) **CHORD TONES**. A lick from **IMPROV STUDY B** (IMPROVISATION STUDY B) is also included.

▶ If you bypassed the ADVANCED IMPROVISATION STUDIES on page 45, you may be unfamiliar with some of the chords and scales used in this solo. Review the ADVANCED IMPROVISATION STUDIES to learn more about these musical elements, or simply use the solo's pitches, rhythms, and licks as a starting point for your own improvisation.

Warm-Ups

1 Chorale
2 Blues Scale Study
C Blues Scale (Concert Bb Blues)
G Blues Scale (Concert F Blues)
3 Dmi7 Study (Concert Cmi7)
D Dorian Scale
Dmi7 Chord Tones
Dmi7 Chord
4 Emi7 Study (Concert Dmi7)
E Dorian Scale
Emi7 Chord Tones
Emi7 Chord
5 Ami7 Study (Concert Gmi7)
A Dorian Scale
Ami7 Chord Tones
Ami7 Chord
6 Gmi7 Study (Concert Fmi7)
G Dorian Scale
Gmi7 Chord Tones
Gmi7 Chord
7 Cmi7 Study (Concert Bbmi7)
C Dorian Scale
Cmi7 Chord Tones
Cmi7 Chord
8 Ami7 Study (Concert Gmi7)
A Natural Minor Scale
Ami7 Chord Tones
Ami7 Chord

9 — **Emi7 Study (Concert Dmi7)**
E Natural Minor Scale · Emi7 Chord Tones · Emi7 Chord

10 — **G7 Study (Concert F7)**
G Mixolydian Scale · G7 Chord Tones · G7 Chord

11 — **F7 Study (Concert Eb7)**
F Mixolydian Scale · F7 Chord Tones · F7 Chord

12 — **D7 Study (Concert C7)**
D Mixolydian Scale · D7 Chord Tones · D7 Chord

13 — **Cma7 Study (Concert Bbma7)**
C Lydian Scale · Cma7 Chord Tones · Cma7 Chord

Scale Glossary

Chord Example (C root)	Scales Used with This Chord	Compared to Major Scale with Same Tonic Note
Cmi7	Most common: Dorian Scale	3rd scale degree down a half step 7th scale degree down a half step
	Alternate: Natural Minor Scale (Aeolian)	3rd scale degree down a half step 6th scale degree down a half step 7th scale degree down a half step
	▸ Blues scales are sometimes used when soloing over minor seventh chords.	
C7	Most common: Mixolydian Scale	7th scale degree down a half step
	▸ Blues scales are sometimes used when soloing over dominant seventh chords.	
Cma7	Most common: Major Scale (Ionian)	————————
	Alternate: Lydian Scale	4th scale degree up a half step

STANDARD OF EXCELLENCE

Jazz Library

The complete curriculum for jazz instruction.

JAZZ ENSEMBLE METHOD

ADVANCED JAZZ ENSEMBLE METHOD

JAZZ COMBO SESSION

JAZZ IN CONCERT SERIES

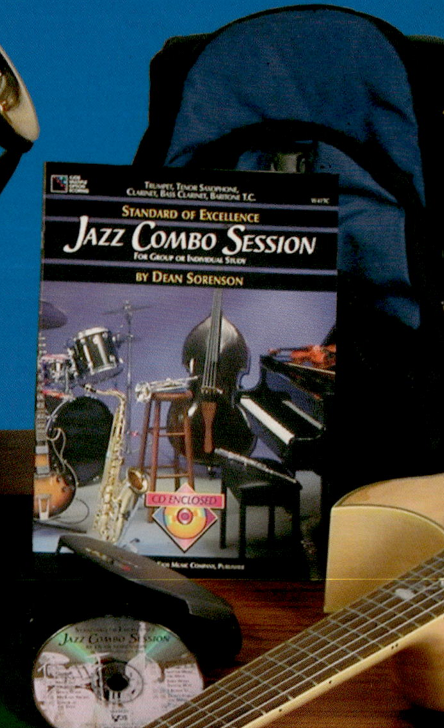

NEIL A. KJOS
MUSIC COMPANY
PUBLISHER

ISBN 0-8497-2556-9

W35TP2 1495

9 780849 725562

90000>